MR. MEN
A Christmas Pantomime

Roger Hargreaves

Original concept by
Roger Hargreaves

Written and illustrated by
Adam Hargreaves

EGMONT

Little Miss Trouble is a real handful.

A real handful of trouble.

And there is no time when she is more of a handful than at Christmas.

There are just so many chances for Little Miss Trouble to cause trouble.

Last Christmas, Little Miss Trouble pinched a slice of Little Miss Neat's Christmas cake and blamed it on Mr Greedy.

Little Miss Neat was not very happy with Mr Greedy.

She told Little Miss Splendid that Mr Quiet had said she looked like a Christmas tree in that hat.

Little Miss Splendid was not very happy with Mr Quiet.

And Little Miss Trouble sent Mr Chatterbox a huge gobstopper pretending it was a Christmas present from Little Miss Chatterbox.

Needless to say, the Chatterboxes' Christmas was not as chatty as usual.

So when it came to the auditions for Little Miss Bossy's Christmas pantomime, Aladdin, it will come as no surprise to hear that she did not get a part.

"I know what you're like," said Little Miss Bossy, "you'll just be trouble from start to finish!"

Little Miss Trouble went home in a foul mood.

"Trouble," she muttered to herself. "I'll show her trouble."

Little Miss Bossy was very pleased with the rest of the auditions.

Little Miss Star got the part of Aladdin, Little Miss Sunshine was to play the Princess, Mr Mean would be the Evil Wizard, Mr Small the Genie of the Lamp and Mr Grumpy, a perfect Widow Twankey.

However, Little Miss Bossy was not so pleased once rehearsals got under way.

Someone put itching powder in Widow Twankey's wig.

Someone told the Princess that Aladdin had said
she wasn't pretty enough to be a princess.

Someone put an egg in the Evil Wizard's curly slipper.

Someone glued the lid of the magic lamp shut and the Genie could not get out.

And someone put a mouse in Aladdin's cave and Aladdin proved to be less brave than everyone had assumed.

It was a disaster.

And Little Miss Bossy knew exactly why it had been a disaster. That evening she went round to Little Miss Trouble's house.

"Okay, I give up," said Little Miss Bossy. "You can have a part in the pantomime."

"Truly?" said Little Miss Trouble. "Which part?"

"Just turn up on the opening night and you'll find out," replied Little Miss Bossy.

On the opening night of the pantomime, Little Miss Trouble was so excited that she barely knew what to do with herself.

She turned up early to discover which part she was to play.

Little Miss Trouble couldn't wait to see her costume.

Just before the start of the performance, Little Miss Bossy called the cast together.

"I thought Little Miss Trouble was going to be here tonight," said Little Miss Sunshine.

"Oh, she is," said Little Miss Bossy.

"Where is she?" asked Mr Mean, looking around the dressing room.

Little Miss Bossy grinned.

"Over here," came a muffled reply from the back of the pantomime horse.

"Keep still!" said Little Miss Stubborn at the front.